D1127581

J
GN
SCOOBY

visit us at www.abdopublishing.com

Reinforced library bound edition published in 2012 by Spotlight, a division of the ABDO Group, 8000 West 78th Street, Edina, Minnesota 55439. Spotlight produces high-quality reinforced library bound editions for schools and libraries. Published by agreement with Warner Bros.—A Time Warner Company. The stories, characters, and incidents mentioned are entirely fictional. All rights reserved. Used under authorization.

Printed in the United States of America, Melrose Park, Illinois.
052011
092011

 This book contains at least 10% recycled materials.

RODGERS MEMORIAL LIBRARY

FEB 0 7 2012

$ 15,85

Copyright © 2011 Hanna-Barbera.
SCOOBY-DOO and all related characters and elements are trademarks of and © Hanna-Barbera.
WB SHIELD: ™ & © Warner Bros. Entertainment Inc.
(s11)

Library of Congress Cataloging-in-Publication Data

Strom, Frank.
  Scooby-Doo in Welcome to the jungle / writer, Frank Strom ; penciller, Roberto Barrios. -- Reinforced library bound ed.
     p. cm. -- (Scooby-Doo graphic novels)
  ISBN 978-1-59961-925-5
  1. Graphic novels. I. Scooby-Doo (Television program) II. Title. III. Title: Welcome to the jungle.
  PZ7.7.S79Sb 2011
  741.5'973--dc22
                                2011001374

All Spotlight books are reinforced library bindings and manufactured in the United States of America.

SCOOBY-DOO!
Table of Contents

SMASH

AWW, SO BUSTED...

CRASH

BANG.

LOOKS LIKE THAT CREATURE IS OUT OF COMMISSION.

WE DON'T HAVE TO WORRY ABOUT IT ANYMORE BECAUSE...

...BEHIND ALL THIS WAX ISN'T A MASKED PERSON, BUT...

...A ROBOT!

AND A BROKEN, REMOTE-CONTROLLED ROBOT, AT THAT.

VELMA'S
MONSTERS
OF THE WORLD
—
THE CALCHONA

john rozum – writer
scott neely – artist

heroic age – colorist
travis lanham – letterer
jeanine schaefer – editor

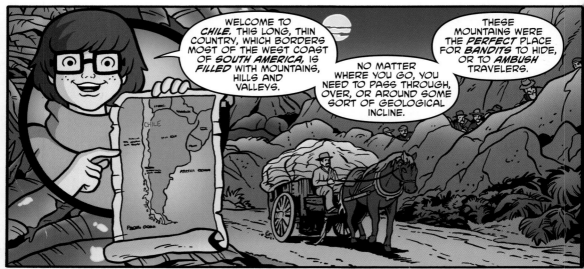

WELCOME TO *CHILE.* THIS LONG, THIN COUNTRY, WHICH BORDERS MOST OF THE WEST COAST OF *SOUTH AMERICA,* IS *FILLED* WITH MOUNTAINS, HILLS AND VALLEYS.

NO MATTER WHERE YOU GO, YOU NEED TO PASS THROUGH, OVER, OR AROUND SOME SORT OF GEOLOGICAL INCLINE.

THESE MOUNTAINS WERE THE *PERFECT* PLACE FOR *BANDITS* TO HIDE, OR TO *AMBUSH* TRAVELERS.

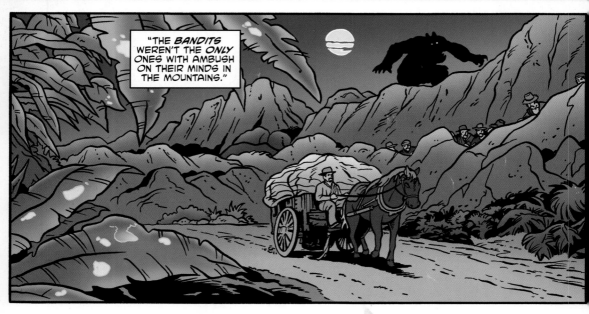

"THE *BANDITS* WEREN'T THE *ONLY* ONES WITH AMBUSH ON THEIR MINDS IN THE MOUNTAINS."

"THE *CALCHONA* BEAST WAS A *HUGE* BEAST *BELIEVED* TO INHABIT MOUNTAIN PASSES, WHO WOULD *SEEK* OUT AND TRAP *TRAVELERS*..."

"...HUNT DOWN OUTLAWS, AND *FRIGHTEN* HORSES."

YOU'D *BETTER* RUN AND HOPE I DON'T *CATCH UP* TO YOU.

HHMPH. IF U'RE GOING MAKE ME GO E TROUBLE CARING YOU THEN YOU D AT LEAST BRING SOME NT FOOD. I EVEN THINK S STUFF IS COOKED.

"WHILE THE CALCHONA GOT UP TO ALL SORTS OF *MISCHIEF*, WHAT IT WAS MOSTLY INTERESTED IN WAS *STEALING* PEOPLE'S *LUNCH BASKETS!*"

RYE KIND OF DOG!

YOUR KIND OF DOG?! THAT FIGURES.

LIKE, DON'T YOU GO GETTING ANY *IDEAS*.

ROO RATE!

?!?!?

LIKE, I SHOULD'VE NAMED YOU SCOOBY-*DON'T*, YOU BIG SANDWICH THIEF!

END

GEORGE H. & ELLA M.
RODGERS MEMORIAL LIBRARY
194 DERRY ROAD
HUDSON, NH 03051